AF606670

INSANE SPEED

DIRT BIKE MANIA

Craig Stevens

A Crabtree Seedlings Book

Crabtree Publishing
crabtreebooks.com

Table of Contents

DIRT BIKE MANIA

What are dirt bikes?

Dirt bikes are **motorcyles** that are made for riding **off-road.**

Dirt bikes are light, fast, and super fun to ride.

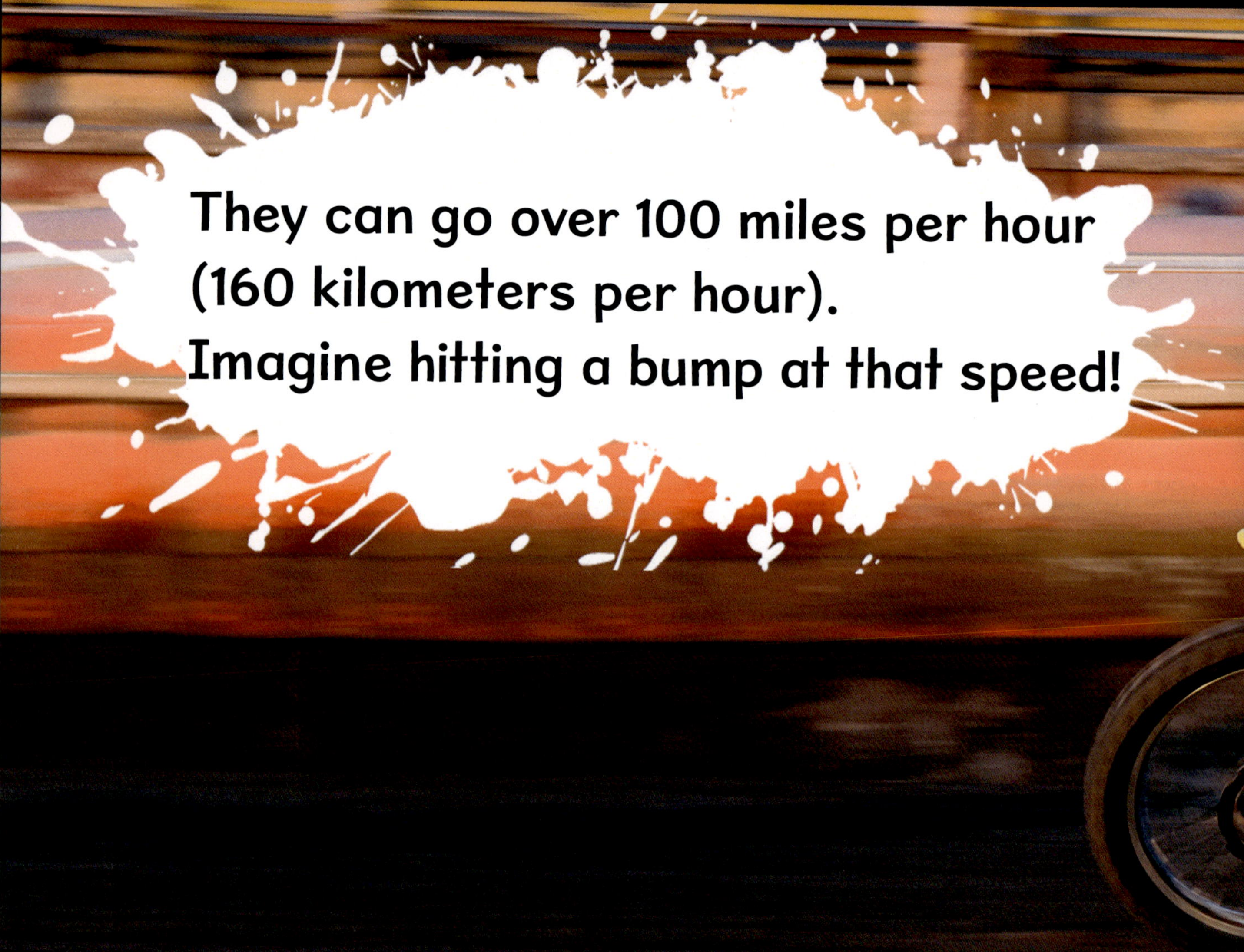

They can go over 100 miles per hour (160 kilometers per hour). Imagine hitting a bump at that speed!

12
PIRELLI
SUZUKI
12

seat - low and narrow
gas tank - holds up to 3 gallons (11 liters) of gas
HONDA
muffler - reduces noise of exhaust being released
chain and sprocket - turns the wheel
engine - small and powerful

handlebars - for steering; also holds controls for the throttle (power), brakes, and clutch to change gears
fender - prevents mud, dirt, and rocks from hitting rider
front shocks - soften hard landings and bumpy ground
knobby tires - bumps give the bike a good grip on the ground
front brakes - stop the bike

Riders **perform** jumps and tricks on dirt bikes.

TOS
320

When a dirt bike lands,
the shocks **absorb** the energy.

Dirt bike tires are called **knobby** tires. They are designed to **grip** dirt, mud, or snow.

Riders can drive dirt bikes through mud and water . . .

. . . over rocks and sand . . .

23
CHAD BAUMAN

. . . over snow and ice!

303

112
57

Glossary

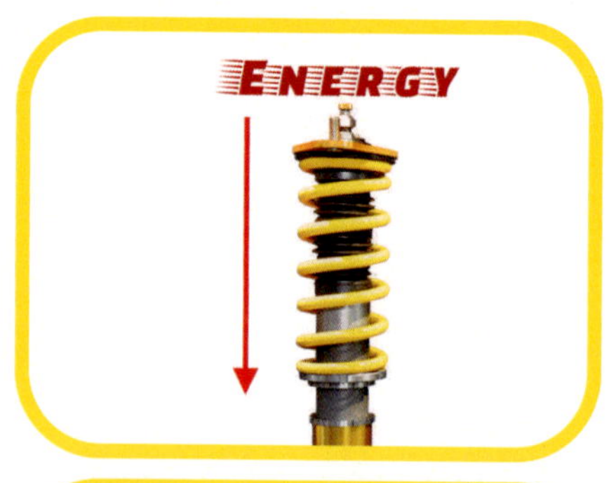

absorb (uhb-ZORB): To take something in or soak up

grip (GRIP): To hold something tightly

knobby (NAHB-ee): Covered in large, rubber bumps

motorcycles (MOH-tur-sye-kuhlz): Vehicles with two wheels and an engine

off-road (OFF-RODE): Made for traveling on rough ground away from public roads

perform (pur-FORM): To do something

Index

School-to-Home Support for Caregivers and Teachers

This book helps children grow by letting them practice reading. Here are a few guiding questions to help the reader build his or her comprehension skills. Possible answers appear here in red.

Before Reading

- **What do I think this book is about?** I think this book is about how much fun it is to ride a dirt bike. I think this book is about all the cool places to ride a dirt bike.
- **What do I want to learn about this topic?** I want to learn more about how to join a dirt bike club. I want to learn about the special equipment needed to ride a dirt bike.

During Reading

- **I wonder why...** I wonder why people like to ride their dirt bikes through mud and water. I wonder why dirt bike riders like to perform tricks.
- **What have I learned so far?** I have learned that off-road means riding on rough ground away from public roads. I have learned that dirt bike tires are designed to grip dirt, mud, or snow.

After Reading

- **What details did I learn about this topic?** I have learned dirt bikes need excellent shock absorbers to help absorb the energy when the rider has a hard landing. I have learned dirt bikes can go over 100 miles per hour (160 km/h).
- **Read the book again and look for the glossary words.** I see the word *absorb* on page 13, and the word *knobby* on page 14. The other glossary words are found on pages 22 and 23.

Crabtree Publishing

crabtreebooks.com 800-387-7650

In Canada: We acknowledge the financial support of the Government of Canada through the Canada Book Fund for our publishing activities.

Hardcover 978-1-0396-4482-3
Paperback 978-1-0396-4673-5

Printed in Canada/102023/CPC20231030

Published in Canada
Crabtree Publishing
616 Welland Avenue
St. Catharines, Ontario
L2M 5V6

Published in the United States
Crabtree Publishing
347 Fifth Avenue
Suite 1402-145
New York, NY 10016

Written by: Craig Stevens

Photo Credits: istock.com, shutterstock.com, Grafikactiva,. COVER: Artur Didyk; Title page: ermess- shutterstock.com; Pages 2-3: homydesign; Pages 4-5: Eugene_Onischenko; Pages 6-7: SDivin09; Pages 8-9: Honda.com; Pages 10-11: Eugene_Onischenko; Pages 12-13: ermess- shutterstock.com; Pages 14-15: Toa55, Holy Polygon; Pages: 16-17: sportpoint; Pages: 18-19: RobertHoetink; Pages 20-21: sportpoint, Edijs Volcjoks; Pages 22-23: intst, yanik88, mahroch, SpeedPhoto.

Library and Archives Canada Cataloguing in Publication
Available at the Library and Archives Canada

Library of Congress Cataloging-in-Publication Data
Available at the Library of Congress